# FOR OUR SON LOGAN...

# "LET THE WORLD HEAR YOU ROAR"

WHEN LOGAN THE LION
WOKE UP IN THE MORNING...
HE STRETCHED AND LET OUT
A BIG ROAR!

# RRROOOAAARRRR

WHEN LOGAN THE LION BRUSHED HIS TEETH... HE GRABBED HIS TOOTHBRUSH AND LET OUT A BIG ROAR!

# RRROOOAAAARRRR

WHEN LOGAN THE LION
GOT DRESSED...
HE PUT ON HIS FAVORITE
SHIRT AND LET OUT
A BIG ROAR!

# RRROOOAAAARRRR

WHEN LOGAN THE LION
ATE BREAKFAST...
HE CHOSE HIS FAVORITE
FRUIT AND LET OUT
A BIG ROAR!

# RRROOOAAAARRRR

WHEN LOGAN THE LION
WENT TO SCHOOL...
HE RODE THE BUS WITH HIS
FRIENDS AND LET OUT
A BIG ROAR!

# RRROOOAAAARRRR

WHEN LOGAN THE LION PLAYED OUTSIDE... HE DRIBBLED THE BASKETBALL AND LET OUT A BIG ROAR!

# RRROOOAAAARRRR

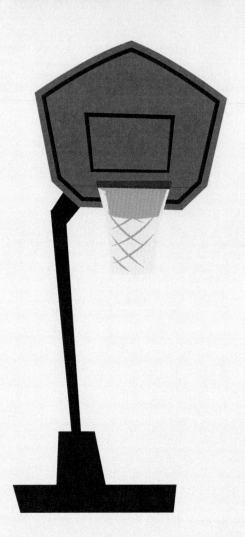

WHEN LOGAN THE LION
DID HIS HOMEWORK...
HE SHARPENED HIS PENCIL
AND LET OUT A BIG ROAR!

# RRROOOAAARRRR

WHEN LOGAN THE LION
TOOK A BATH...
HE WASHED HIS HAIR
AND LET OUT A BIG ROAR!

# RRROOOAAAARRRR

WHEN LOGAN THE LION
WENT TO BED...
HE SAID GOOD NIGHT TO
HIS MAMA AND PAPA
AND LET OUT A SLEEPY
LITTLE ROAR!

45297821R00015

Made in the USA
Middletown, DE
15 May 2019